Rendezvous
with Life

A Poetry Collection Celebrating the Beauty of Life

Devika Das

Ukiyoto Publishing

All global publishing rights are held by

Ukiyoto Publishing

Published in 2023

Content Copyright © Devika Das

ISBN 9789358466904

*All rights reserved.
No part of this publication may be reproduced, transmitted, or stored in a retrieval system, in any form by any means, electronic, mechanical, photocopying, recording or otherwise, without the prior permission of the publisher.*

The moral rights of the authors have been asserted.

This is a work of fiction. Names, characters, businesses, places, events, locales, and incidents are either the products of the author's imagination or used in a fictitious manner. Any resemblance to actual persons, living or dead, or actual events is purely coincidental.

This book is sold subject to the condition that it shall not by way of trade or otherwise, be lent, resold, hired out or otherwise circulated, without the publisher's prior consent, in any form of binding or cover other than that in which it is published.

www.ukiyoto.com

Dedicated to my parents

Contents

Lull before the storm	1
Perspective	2
City of Nizams	3
Death Know Not Thee	5
Death, I Know Not Thee	6
Preserve Humanity	7
For Those At Kargil	9
Smile	11
Isn't it true?	13
The Morning Sky	14
Life	15
Life of a Tree	16
Child Labour	17
About the Author	18

Lull before the storm

The silence is deafening,
Scarred thoughts bruise the mind.
Trauma becomes real.
Look into the mirror.
Ask yourself.
What if the perpetrator wins?
Would you walk away with a smile?
Or, vow for vengeance?
The strong walks out without a fuss.
The perpetrator shines in false glory
Once, you brave the situation
The cold war ends.
Seems like a storm in the teacup.
It is just like a passing phase
Temporary states don't stay forever.
Congratulate the perpetrator as nothing is lost.
Right intent will be conveyed to the Universe.
For due justice and wisdom to prevail.

Perspective

Fickle minds, multiple distractions
The constant chatter in our mind
PoV is unique and so is perspective
Don't judge but understand,
Coz empathy is all that the world needs.
The difference of opinion is obvious
But respecting it is essential, for building harmony
Life is all about perspective, it turns around with experiences
Step out of your own and see the world view.
Make perspective your prison or your hope
As it depends on where you stand.

City of Nizams

The City of Nizams,
gifts warmth and calm.

Palatial structures, rocky bends
Add to its beauty and charm.

The sun illuminates Qutub Shahi Tombs
Golconda Fort stands firm and tall.

Majestic aura of Chowmahalla
Vintage cars of Falaknuma.

Magnificence of the Charminar
Glistening bangles of Laad Bazaar.

The ever-famous pearls market
Is a must-visit and not to miss.

Peacocks dance around lush greens of KBR Park
The expanse of blue at Hussain Sagar.

Musical clock of Salar Jung strikes twelve,
The cicerone has a different story to tell.

Ramoji Film City – a traveller's feast
Where oceans of aesthetics meet.

Treasure trove of knowledge at Abids' Book Market
Lamakaan – the creative's perfect asset.

Warmth of the people,
Offers everyone a cuddle.

Intoxicating aroma of Irani chai
Biryani and Haleem in every lane.

Ah! a week-long stay in Hyderabad
Offers memories to cherish forever.

Death Know Not Thee

The last breath of yours
Fills me with remorse.
What you mean for me,
I understand now.
My angel, please don't go
My world will become hell.
With your absence,
Life's charm will fade.
Death knows not thee,
Your meaning in my life.
Love will disappear
This void can't be filled.

Death, I Know Not Thee

Death, I know not thee.
My spirit's happy and free
Fear doesn't haunt me
Darkness embraces me.
Failure can't discourage
Always strive to move ahead
Heart doesn't beat in a straight line
Complexities of life are simply fine.
Accept challenges with open arms
Fear of death can do no harm
Monotony is a curse,
Vibrancy fills life with colours.
Death, I know not thee
You fail to attract me.

Preserve Humanity

Running the rat race, I always wondered
How time passed like quicksand?
Hourly conversations with good pals,
Confined to SMSes and forwards.
Greeting people on social occasions,
A rarity now.

People's memories begin to fade,
even before they get salt peppery hair.
What legacy do we leave behind?
Where man-machine is hyped,
Real relationships defied.
People anxious for virtual appreciation,
Real comments shunned as interference.

Don't ask me about patience or tolerance;
New gen sees them as trivial.
Screen time is most cherished,

Off-screen leaves one idle and bored.
Now or Never, chants echo around,
But path to Now is rarely tread.
Erstwhile luxury - the new basic need
Mercy and empathy - possessions of the weak.
Are we really progressing?

For Those At Kargil

My heart bleeds, my soul cries
Each time up there a soldier dies.
Fighting the cold, braving the snow
They trudge ahead, fearlessly.

No one knows if they'll come back
No one knows how long it'll be.
He had hardly lived life
Before he had to face death.
But he was glad
Promise to the nation he had kept.

In another town, another place
The four- year-old lights his father's pyre
He perhaps doesn't even know that
There'll be no more Papa whom he admired.

Parents watch news anxiously

And so does his young wife
But, their prayers go unanswered
When they hear he's laid down his life.

There are many more, so many of them
Unsung heroes, these courageous men.
I salute you all, who for our tomorrow
Sacrificed your today, left us in sorrow
Let this end, let there be peace
God! Will you fulfil this wish of mine, please?

Smile

Just a little smile cheers your heart
The day goes well when with a smile it starts
Keeps you in good humour, preserves peace in your soul
Gives the force to try and move towards your goal
Enhances good health, beautifies your face
Mightier than a sword and powerful than a mace.
It can change a tyrant into a man tame
It gives speech to the dumb and limbs to the lame
It induces kind thoughts, to perform kind deeds
It's a basic ingredient, each human needs
It reduces tension and relieves all pain
Whether you use it or others do, we're all to gain.
Brings new hope in the lives of the weary
Gives courage to tread lands scary
Increases when shared, cannot be divided
It can neither be bought nor provided
Neither the giver loses, nor the receiver wins
It's just a chance to get rid of all sins.

Bridges all gaps as it is a 'mile' long.
Gives brightness to colour, adds melody to a song
Gives a shine to the face that shares a laugh along
It's a sign of pure, innocent mind
Makes all cheerful around you
Makes others smile and release their problems too
With a smile on your face, you can cross all barriers
It is the real wealth we can truly call ours.

Isn't it true?

If a student doesn't work hard, the teacher criticizes

If a person fails, he considers himself as inferior

Joys seem sweeter, if they come after many sorrows?

Rain after scorching summer heat, makes people dance to music and beat.

It is true.

Life's full of surprises

Giving success to those, whom society criticizes

Life is full of hardships/constraints

Real winner tackles them without any restraint.

The Morning Sky

The sun rises, behind the hills of the East.
Gives the early riser's eyes a visual feast.
Breathtaking scenery all around.
From the clouds, bright colours rebound.
Birds chirping, fly higher
Make it seem as if the air is lighter
Morning sky, seen at a glance
Makes million hearts prance.
Each morning, fresh and new.
How oft witness'd such a scene did you?

Life

Life is a battle of mind and ego
Where one faces joy and sorrow
Great ones' steps you must follow
Never make your dreams hollow.
Life's a challenge everyone faces
One is poor, other is rich.
It's not easy to live life
As only the fittest survive.

Life of a Tree

From a sapling, I begin my journey.
Dream to see the whole world
The wind, sun, rain challenge my strength
My roots help me stick to the ground.

Chirping birds perch on my branch.
Look the sun at a glance
The shade one enjoys out of my leaves
Sigh of relief, everyone heaves.

Dry leaves shed in autumn,
 Fill my heart with despair
New leaves give me hope.
Horizons with a wider scope.

Child Labour

A new born child is free
Fills parents' hearts with glee
Well wishers shower blessings
May he live long and a be a good human being.

But at 7, he works hard with Dad,
As family condition is bad.
Fate thinks otherwise, and hands him tools
Agonizingly longing for school.

About the Author

Devika Das

An award-winning poet and a bestselling author, Devika Das has 3 publications under her name. Her title 'The Mind Game' has received appreciation from India and abroad, and is a national bestseller. She has participated in key literary events at Hyderabad and around India as well. Besides writing, Devika pursues her passion for Acting and is an active theatre artiste in Hyderabad and has featured in several short films. Presently, she is associated with Nishumbita School of Drama, Hyderabad and is the Director of Navarasa, the Theatre wing of The NRB.

An avid writer and author of multiple books, Devika has also edited two books (a novel called Absolute Love Letter and a business fiction book called Diamonds In The Rough).

Creative writing liberates her and is a medium that allows her to reveal her true SELF. Within few years into book publishing, her literary works have received critical acclaim through several award nominations and book launch events in several cities of India. Professionally, she is a full-time Marketing Lead in Cognida.ai, Hyderabad.

www.ingramcontent.com/pod-product-compliance
Lightning Source LLC
LaVergne TN
LVHW041644070526
838199LV00053B/3550